The Bride Thief

KENDALL HAWKINS, ISABELLA STARLING

Cover design: Kendall Hawkins, Isabella Starling

Editing: John Hudspith

Contents

To the dark addictions we all fight.

From The Author

My dearest reader,

Welcome to my dark, twisted and depraved world. Be aware the book you're holding doesn't hold back on the darkness. If sensitive subject matter upsets you, please don't read further.

The Bride Thief is the prequel of the Dark Vows duet. All books must be read in order and are not standalones.

Dark Vows Duet:

#0.5 The Bride Thief

#1 The Wife Breaker

#2 The Widow Maker

You can also sign up for my newsletter for freebies, ARC opportunities and cover reveals.

Kendall.

Blurb

One taste gave me an addiction for life.

We were promised to one another as children.

Heath took my first kiss and stole my innocence.

He wrote me letters filled with love, darkness, and hope.

I was supposed to be his wife, until everything I knew was ripped away from me.

My life is over and there's no one who can help me now.

Not even the boy with charcoal eyes...

The Bride Thief is the short prequel to the Dark Vows duet. It is not a standalone book.

Prologue

RAIN

ONCE UPON A TIME...

He is only *just* a man, but his dark eyes convey a quiet understanding of the world I don't yet possess.

Heath Gunn is a dark-haired young boy with slanted eyes the color of charcoal.

He is tanned and beautiful, already promising to grow into a tall, dark and dangerous man.

His hair is slightly too long, in need of a haircut; he keeps pushing it back from his already chiseled face.

His thick, voluminous lashes are spidery, long and pitch-black, resting on full cheeks as he closes his eyes and searches for another flower in the field of weeds, using merely his touch to guide him.

I watch his hand moving across the blades of grass and wheat, mesmerized.

I want to impress him. I want him to like me.

Eagerly, I scan the field for a blossom.

"Here's one!"

I pluck the poppy flower out of the cracked and overheated ground. The land doesn't grow much here, apart from wheat and the poppies. Nana and I have to water it so the plants don't die in the oppressive heat.

Nana told me a poppy is merely a weed, but I refuse to believe something so beautiful could be useless.

Nana also said it was a parasite. That it kills the other plants in the field. I don't care about that, either.

It's the most beautiful flower that grows here, and if it had to kill to dominate this field, well, that's just natural selection at its finest.

My eyes wander over Heath's soft but pronounced features through which a man is already emerging. His expression darkens, a line appearing on his forehead and creasing his unmarred skin.

I am so enthralled by the boy in front of me, I would do anything to impress him. *Anything*.

My fingers tremble as I pass him the freshly picked flower.

He takes it without allowing his olive-toned skin to touch mine, thoughtfully watching the frail petals as his gentle fingertips touch the paper-thin flower. Once again, I'm mesmerized, as he gently traces his fingers along the petals.

Before I can stop him, his fingers suddenly wrap in a fist around the bud. He crushes it between his fingers, and I gasp, shocked at how easily he can destroy something so beautiful.

"Why did you do that?" I ask him, doing my best so my tone won't betray my unseemly insecurities.

He looks right at me as he responds, those charcoal eyes burning with fire and threatening to ignite me.

"Because I can do anything I want."

The boy I thought so innocent and pure is no longer. In his wake, he's left behind a cold, emotionless barely-human beast who seems much too grown up for his tender age. And yet the thought of this crueler version of Heath only excites me more.

Absentmindedly, I allow my fingertips to wander over the blades of bone-dry grass in the field.

Sooner rather than later, Nana will come out to get us and Heath will have to go back home. But I don't want to see him go. I'm hoping I can steal a few more minutes of his time and put my mark on the morning we spent together. I'm desperate for our encounter to mean something to him. I want him to remember me... I want his mind racing with thoughts of my face, my words, my voice. Because I already know that's going to happen to me once he walks away from Nana's cottage.

The remains of the crushed poppy flower are still on the ground when Nana and the boy's guardian appear on the dirt path in front of our stone cottage. Heath picks himself up and turns around.

While he's distracted, I hurriedly sweep up the remains of the destroyed poppy and gently place them in the pocket of my checkered black-and-white dress. The memory of Heath's punishing fist crushing the petals is still fresh in my mind, and for some inexplicable reason, I'm eager to hold on to a memento of what just happened.

"We should be getting back. Are you coming?"

The boy turns to face me, his nearly black eyes lightening until I can see specks of amber in them in the morning sun. He's so beautiful, almost out of this world.

I pick myself up and nod, dusting off my dress to make sure I still look presentable for Heath's guardian. Heath's an orphan, just like me. Perhaps that's why we share a connection – because the same heart-wrenching pain tore our lives apart.

I suppose we're just two wildflowers in a field, like the poppies. We're trying to survive in an unkind environment. Perhaps if things work out, our roots will intertwine in the earth and we'll grow stronger together as one.

"You have something in your hair."

Heath reaches forward and I flinch when his fingertips make contact with the strands of my dirty blonde hair. He pulls his hand back and he knits his brows together as he watches me with newfound interest.

"Are you afraid of me?"

I worry my bottom lip between my teeth. How am I supposed to answer his question? Yes, there is a part of me that fears him – the part that knows one day I will answer only to him, and he will likely be as merciless as he was with the flower I gave him. After all, it's his job to keep me safe, secure and obedient. I can't exactly blame him for that. It's expected of me, given my position. There's no room for arguments in my life. I learned that the hard way.

"Answer me."

"I am not afraid of you." The words roll off my tongue before I can stop them. "I'm not afraid of *anything*."

"That seems unwise," he mutters while I delight in the pleasure of his melodic voice.

"You're a foolish little girl. And you still have something in your hair."

Self-consciously, I drag my fingers through my hair, but Heath clicks his tongue impatiently.

"Not there. Let me."

He takes a step forward and my stomach does a somersault as he makes contact again. This time, the boy allows his fingers to roam over my pale skin, leaving a searing heat in his wake. If this is what being touched by a boy feels like, I finally understand why Nana has been warning me about it my whole life.

He seems preoccupied by touching me, and his brows furrow even more when his fingers finally travel into my hair. He tugs something free, pulling out a twig from my mane of hair. I blush, embarrassed at the thought of him seeing me in such a disarray. I spent my whole life preparing for this very moment. And now all he's going to remember of me is that I'm the girl whose hair is a nest filled with grass and twigs, like a savage, wild animal.

I raise my eyes to his and force myself to stop the tears from falling.

"You don't like *me*, do you?"

"I never said that," Heath shakes his head before sighing, running a hand through his dark mop of hair. The gesture makes him appear troubled, adding years to his age.

"Don't put words in my mouth."

Tears of frustration well in my eyes. I wanted to impress him. Now everything is ruined.

"Don't cry. I don't like it."

I shake my head wordlessly, unable to come up with a reply as more tears slide down my cheeks. It's not just this interaction, it's the fact that I'll eventually have to leave Nana's side to be with this boy who clearly hates me.

"I told you not to cry." Heath looks troubled as our eyes meet.

"I can't help it," I mutter.

"You should," he responds. "You shouldn't wear your emotions on your sleeve like that. It's not befitting for my wife."

Despite everything, the words make my heart race. And yet the tears still won't stop.

With a frustrated groan, Heath reaches for me and grabs me by the waist. He pulls me closer. The world is at a standstill as his strong hand reaches my face and his thumb smudges the tear on my cheek.

"Maybe I do like it after all," he mutters, more to himself than me.

I flush as he raises his thumb to his lips and sucks it into his mouth, tasting the saltiness of my tears.

"You look pretty when you cry, Rain."

Our eyes meet and we burn together for several excruciatingly long moments. Before I can say another word, Heath closes the distance between us and suddenly captures my lips in a kiss.

I cry out in protest but don't fight back. His palms go to my cheeks and he pulls me in, deepening the no longer innocent kiss. My heart is beating so fast it feels like I'll be knocked unconscious any second, but it's not enough to dissuade Heath, who surely feels it hammering between us.

And then the kiss is over. He pulls back, the remains of my innocence on his lips. I swallow thickly, needing more but so very scared at the same time I don't dare say a word. The moment is gone and all that's left are my memories, tainted by my fear of this savage boy.

I half-expect him to apologize, but when he doesn't, I cross my arms and mutter, "You weren't supposed to do that."

"You weren't supposed to cry like a baby," he growls at me. "How are you going to handle marriage if the smallest insult makes you cry?"

"You shouldn't be insulting me at all." My eyes flash with anger. "You should be giving me compliments."

He laughs out loud, shaking his head, but I keep staring at him with determination.

"Seriously?"

"Yeah." I cock my head to the side. "I'm waiting."

"Your hair is the color of the fields," Heath says slowly. "Golden, like wheat."

I don't know what to make of his words. Unsure whether or not it's truly a compliment, I tuck my hair behind my ear and give him a shy smile. "Was that so hard? Thank you."

"Come on, Goldilocks. We need to go back."

His nickname for me makes me flush, but I do my best not to show it. I nod instead, scrambling for the right words to finish our conversation but coming up empty again and again. Eagerness to leave an impression leaves me speechless, and before I know it, Nana yells out for us.

"We should go." Heath nods toward the small house amid the fields. "My guardian will be waiting."

Sheepishly, I fall into step behind him, taking every opportunity I have left to study him, the way he walks, the way he glances over his shoulder to make sure I'm still following him.

"Hurry up," he mutters. "We don't want to keep them waiting, they'll be angry."

I've never in my life seen Nana angry with me, but I nod as if I know what he's talking about. We reach the cottage where Nana and Heath's guardian are waiting. A little way off, an expensive, lacquered black car is waiting. Two armed guards stand in front of it. I know they're here to keep us safe, but the sight of them, loaded with weapons, only makes me shiver with fear.

"You're sure you weren't followed?" Nana asks Heath's guardian while I take the opportunity to swallow the man up with my eyes, trying to decide whether I'm scared of h

"Do you take me for an amateur, Mathilda?" the man barks in return. "Of course we weren't followed. We have the boy's safety to think of."

"And I have my granddaughter to protect," Nana bites back.

I can hardly hide my smile. Nana never lets a man treat her this way. She's the confident, resilient woman I aspire to be one day.

"Her life is just as important as your nephew's, as I'm sure you'll acknowledge, Xavier."

"Let's not compare whose life is more important," Xavier bites back. "That's not a battle you're ever going to win."

"Because my granddaughter is a girl?" Nana gives the rude man one of her signature, hearty laughs. "You forget how valuable she is to you, Xavier. After all, she'll give your boy the heir he so desperately needs, won't she?"

"Let's not get ahead of ourselves," Heath's guardian mutters, sizing me up again. "She looks thin as a reed. Certainly too thin to birth a child. Those hips are too narrow. Have you been feeding her enough?"

"She's sixteen years old," Nana fights back. "She's grown six inches this year. Give her some time to fill out."

Perhaps some other girl would be offended about being spoken about this way, but I'm not. Since I came to live with Nana when my parents died, I've known my purpose. Nana never hid it from me and I was grateful for that – it made it easier to accept what my life would become.

Heath has been awfully quiet through this whole exchange, and while Xavier barks orders at his guards, I take my time to examine the boy one last time. It might be my last chance... after all, they made this visit specifically to meet me, and there's a high possibility the next time I see Heath will be at our wedding day.

He's staring at his guardian with an emotion I can't quite place. There's something in those slanted, charcoal eyes that scares me and fills me with trepidation. But at least it's not directed at me – no, Heath is staring right at his guardian with something akin to contempt in his gaze.

But why would he hate Xavier? The man is the only reason Heath is still alive, and he bears the scars to prove it.

"Heath, we're leaving," Xavier says, striding toward their expensive car. "Come now, don't dawdle."

"Not yet." Heath is only a few years older than me but he speaks in a calm, quiet way that makes it clear he's the boss here despite his tender age. "I have a question for Mrs. Ferrell."

"It's Miss," Nana harrumphs.

I can't help but smile. She loves to remind people she's never been married.

"Miss Ferrell," Heath smiles, visibly amused by her correction. "I wanted to ask whether you'd allow me to send your granddaughter some letters. As we both know, the chance of us seeing each other again before the wedding is unlikely. I know it's unorthodox, but..."

He glances at me thoughtfully, and I feel myself flushing deeply.

"I would like to stay in contact with Rain, if that's alright with you."

"Why?" Nana demands, her eyes narrowing in suspicion while my heart beats into overdrive.

Oh please, Nana. *Please* let me have this. I'm already eager for more of this mysterious boy whose side I will stand by when I get older. I want those letters. I want to stay in touch. I want to know what we could become.

"Arranged marriages can be taxing on young women," Heath replies, speaking much like an adult. "I want Rain to be comfortable with our union once she says I do. And I'd like to get to know her better."

Nana smirks and wipes her flour-covered hands on her apron. It's made of the same fabric as my dress. Nana makes all our clothes and food, and her hands are permanently covered in flour from baking loaves of bread for us. Now, she reaches forward and Heath shakes her hand, disregarding the remnants of the white powder on her palms.

"You have a deal, young man," she nods her approval.

"Heath," Xavier interrupts, groaning with displeasure. "Car. *Now*."

"Coming, Xavier."

Reluctantly, Heath turns to face me one last time. I force myself to commit every one of his features to memory. I'll be grateful for it later, when all that will be left to remember him will be the crushed poppy flower in my pocket.

"I'm glad to have met you, Rain."

"Likewise," I whisper, my voice breaking over the simple word.

Something dark flashes across Heath's face again, but he doesn't say anything else, merely turns around and gets into the dark car with tinted windows.

Xavier gets in the vehicle after him while Nana comes to stand behind me, her hands coming to rest on my shoulders.

"He seems like a nice boy," she says softly as the car pulls away, driving back onto the dirt road and toward the next village which is an hour's drive away. "Did you like him, Rain?"

"Yes," I whisper, staring into the distance where the car is getting smaller and smaller.

Heath's charcoal eyes are on my mind, as well as his calm manner and the darkness that only I seemed to notice.

"He is a nice boy."

"He will make a good husband," Nana continues, her fingers lightly digging into my shoulder. "Your parents would approve."

I nod numbly, trusting her enough to believe what she's saying. There's no way for me to know whether she's telling the truth. My parents died long ago, and I don't remember them.

The life I know is here.

Amidst the wheat fields the same color as my hair, with Nana, with loaves of freshly baked sourdough bread and blood red wild poppies that will now forever remind me of Heath Gunn – the boy I will one day be forced to marry.

My fingers wrap around the drying poppy flower in the pocket of my dress, and I repeat Heath's motion, crushing it even more until my fingers come away stained with redness.

I wonder whether it's a premonition of what's to come next.

Chapter One

RAIN

TODAY IS MY EIGHTEENTH birthday, but truly, it's just like any other day in *Nana*'s cottage amid the golden fields.

I carry a pail to the stone well behind the house. It's gotten easier to handle it as the years go by. I still remember when I was just a little girl, struggling to lift it with every step when it was filled up with ice-cold water from the well. But not anymore – now I've grown strong and tall. My once stick-thin figure has filled out, and Nana has told me I'm becoming a woman. I don't know whether that scares or excites me.

I hook the pail onto the chain, sitting down on the edge of the well. Looking deep into the abyss, I wonder just how deep the well really is, but the thought chills me. Instead of dwelling on it, I slowly lower the pail more and more until I hear it hit the water below me. I repeat the process I know by heart now, filling up the bucket and slowly lifting it back out so I don't over-exert my already tired muscles.

Perhaps other girls get to spend their entry into adulthood differently, but I don't. Not with *Nana* watching. I smile at the thought. She's always so eager to make me work hard. She says that's the only way I'll appreciate everything that's given to me in life. And I'm not complaining... it's just that life in *Nana*'s cottage gets lonely. I long for a companion, a friend or even a cat to keep me company. But there's nobody here but *Nana* and me.

Up until a few months ago, there was something else. The thick stack of handwritten letters next to my cot tells a story of a boy infatuated with me, just as much as I am with him.

Heath Gunn kept his promise. When *Nana* handed me the first letter, I was shocked he'd remembered and kept his word. But soon enough, I discovered Heath never lied when it came to promises. His word was as good as sacred.

As the years passed, the envelopes carrying Heath's letters got thicker and heavier. His words spilled on the paper with shocking honesty and surprising clarity, giving me a glimpse into the life of a boy who was not happy at all.

The letters came every few months, then weeks. I waited impatiently for the days Nana left for the village, a six hour walk away from our stone cottage. She never allowed me to come with her, and I knew better than to argue with her. It was too dangerous, and I needed to stay hidden to protect my life. But I lived for those village days, long, drawn out and soaked in the scorching hot sun. As day turned into dusk, Nana would come back from the village, weary, tired, but nevertheless with a smile on her face as she pulled her canvas bag open and pulled out a new stack of letters from my husband-to-be.

I would reply dutifully, writing pages upon pages of thoughts, observations and my most hidden secrets for Heath to peruse. Perhaps it was easier to be so open since I never got to see him face to face. The words spilled upon the paper easily, and I was eager to uncover all my secrets for Heath to read.

But then, two-hundred-and-seven days ago, the letters stopped coming.

I still remember the first time Nana came back from the village without a single envelope. How my bottom lip trembled, how my brows knitted together in worry. Because Heath never missed a letter. I always had at least a few waiting. But not this time. Nana's hands were empty, and she seemed as disappointed as I was.

Since then, there has been no letter at all. It's left me to wonder why Heath is no longer in touch. Perhaps he doesn't want me anymore. Perhaps his guardian has forbidden him from writing to me. Perhaps he's fallen for someone else. The last thought hurts the most, twisting my stomach into painful knots that remind me we haven't seen one another in years – apart from the letters, I'm a stranger to Heath.

Once the pail is pulled back up, I snap out of my thoughts and unhook it from the chain. Balancing my weight, I begin carrying it back to the cottage, so we have our daily supply of water, but my mind is still lingering on the past, eager to cling on to any memories I have left of him.

Those letters are falling apart, the ink smudging from the amount of times my fingertips glided over the words, memorizing them all. And now I'm eighteen, and we haven't had word from the Gunns yet.

I trip on a pebble in the cracked ground and groan as some water spills over the edge of my bucket. My eyes fly up and what I see instantly sends my heart racing.

There is a car parked in front of Nana's cottage. I have only seen one car here before– a black, lacquered long one with tinted windows. And while this one isn't the exact same, it certainly looks similar.

Is it possible they've finally come to collect me?

The pail drops from my hands, but I'm too far gone to worry about the precious water seeping into the dry ground. My attention is on the dirt path leading up to Nana's cottage, and on the three men that have now emerged from the shiny black car.

The other two men must be guards.

I start walking toward the cottage as if in a trance as the old wooden door opens and Nana comes outside into the hot, scorching sun. She's wiping her hands on her apron and I smile to myself, knowing they're streaked with traces of flour yet again.

Nana's mouth moves as she starts speaking to the men, but I'm too far away to hear what she's saying. I stride forward, watching the car closely and trying to see if Heath will come out soon, too. But there's no sign of him.

Then, a loud bang rings out in the open fields and I drop to my knees, scuffing them raw on the hard ground beneath. I press my palms over my ears and groan. My head hurts and my heart is pounding as I look back at the cottage. One of the guards has fired his weapon into the air. But why?

Nana is screaming now, waving her hands. I'm still too far away to hear her words, but not far away enough to miss what happens next.

The guards point their guns at my grandmother and fire several bullets as Xavier Gunn gives them a signal to do so.

My heart stops.

My head spins.

Nana drops to the ground.

Still.

Dead.

The moment replays in my head.

Boom, boom, down. Boom, boom, down. Down, down, *down.*

The scream that rips from my lips is brutal, guttural and animalistic, shocking me to my core. My body shivers and screams for mercy as the gunmen's eyes connect with mine. They begin striding toward me resolutely, while someone yells my name into the dying sun.

"Rain!"

My name echoes in the fields, hunting me, haunting me. It follows me, the words morphing into something else as I pick myself up on bare feet, the pail lying forgotten on the ground.

Rain, Rain, run. Rain, Rain, run. Run, run, *run.*

I trip over my own feet and scream again, my voice quickly becoming ragged and hoarse. But I don't stop trying to get away. All that's left is a self-preservation instinct, and it's stronger than my mind right now, propelling me forward on the sun-scorched earth, even though I know there's nowhere for me to run.

A hand wrapping around my throat stops me in my tracks. Strong fingers squeeze down, preventing me from taking another breath. My vision darkens and I struggle in the vice-like grip to no avail. I'm trapped.

The man slams my body against the dry earth. His wet fingers finally leave my throat and I realize with horror I'm now smeared with blood – Nana's blood. I turn around on the ground, scrambling backward as a figure appears in front of me, basked in the sun that kills anything and everything, but not my Nana. No, that honor goes to the man before me – and now that I can see who it is, my blood runs cold.

"You," I hiss. "What the fuck are you doing?"

"Don't curse," he smirks at me. "It doesn't befit my wife."

"Fuck you." I spit at his feet, staring at him with pure contempt.

"You will." He kneels next to me. His eyes are brown, not the charcoal I crave to see. This isn't Heath – it's his guardian, Xavier. "If you don't obey, I'll cut your tongue out. I don't want a wife that talks back. So, if you know what's good for you, you'll shut the hell up and do as you're told."

"Where's Heath?" I demand, looking for a way out as I'm surrounded by Xavier's men clad in black. Their weapons are pointed at me, and I hiss when one of them nudges me with the barrel of his gun. Xavier tells them to lower their weapons but I still burn with pure hatred for the prick who just ruined my life. "Why did you do that to Nana?"

"Your grandmother was an unfortunate casualty," Xavier mutters. "She had to die. We can't leave any witnesses behind, it's too fucking risky."

"You killed her," I whisper, my voice breaking over the words as the truth finally settles in. "You let her bleed... You took her life... Why?"

"I told you, and I'm not going to repeat myself." The man picks himself up and nods at one of his goons. "Take everything in the cottage, then burn it to the ground."

"No!" I scream. The thought of my life, all my memories, going up in flames, tears me apart.

"Shut up." Xavier kicks the ground, making a dust cloud rise and soliciting a coughing attack from me. "Do it."

Three of the men head to the cottage, leaving me in the dirt with two others and Xavier Gunn.

"Where's Heath?" I demand again.

"Would you shut up already?" Xavier hisses.

"Not until you tell me what you did to him, fucker." I pick myself up and instantly find my forehead pressed against a gun. But it doesn't stop me. I keep glaring at Xavier, my eyes demanding an answer.

"Heath and I... We're not on the best of terms," Xavier says coolly, ordering his goon to lower the gun. "Your wedding is off, as you may have guessed."

"What did you do to him?" I demand. "He was sending me letters and he stopped almost a year ago. I knew something happened. What did you do?"

"Nothing that concerns you." He watches as the guards carry my belongings out of the cottage and into the shiny black car. "Now, I would advise you not to fight us in the process. Or else you're going to regret it really fucking soon."

"What process?" I narrow my eyes, struggling against the two men who've now grabbed me by the forearms and are forcing me to my knees. "What are you going to do, fucking kill me like you did Nana?"

"Don't be fucking stupid." Xavier nods and a syringe appears in one of the guard's hands. I thrash wildly against their grip but it's no use. They're holding on too tightly and I can't break free. "Get it over with, I don't have time for this."

"No!" I scream while the guard plunges the needle into my forearm. "No! Fuck you!"

Nobody pays me any mind. They just let go.

I'm finally free and I jump to my feet, quickly finding my body heavy and tired.

"What did you do to me?" I try to snarl at Xavier, but my words come out muffled. I can barely move my mouth, my tongue is thick and heavy and my eyelids are getting heavier, too. Panicked, I look at the cottage where men are setting fire to Nana's vegetable garden. I want to scream at them, tell them they'll burn down the whole field that way, but I can't even move my lips anymore.

I sink back to my knees, using every last vestige of power to force myself not to fall. I can't let this happen. I can't go down without a fight. I can't let them take everything from me.

But with a sinking feeling, I remind myself they already have, because Nana is dead.

As my body becomes increasingly number, I can only watch as the men set fire to Nana's unmoving body. Flames rise into the sky as my consciousness seeps through my pores, abandoning me in utter darkness where monsters prey.

The ability to move isn't taken from me, it's ripped away, leaving a sore, bloody wound in its wake. I can't even struggle as the men obey Xavier's orders and tie me up with zip ties just to be fucking pricks – there's no way I can move, anyway. They throw me inside their car where the last straws of my consciousness break, sinking into nothing.

My last memory is the smell of burning fields, joined by the stench of flesh charring in the fire they set to my entire life.

Chapter Two

RAIN

WHEN I WAKE UP, I'm somewhere that feels different.

The golden fields had a heat that was hard to get used to. Sharp, dry, and biting, it made every breath ragged.

But the heat in this place is different.

It's thick and oppressive, the air heavy with moisture. It's a wet heat, something I'm entirely unused to, and the first thing I notice when I wake up in a thick, plush bed covered with a mosquito net. I bolt upright, and as my memories come back to me, the pain hits me right in the chest.

Glancing around, I try to adjust to the quickened pace of my heartbeat as I make sense of where I am. The room is large and beautiful, decorated in oak wood and whites. Everything is beige, white, or wooden. It's calming, beautiful. Silk curtains billow at the balcony door in front of which a guard is standing. It instantly becomes clear I am a prisoner.

My lips thin out into a line as I check my forearm. There it is – the puncture mark where that bastard stabbed me with the needle. They drugged me and took me away from the only home I've ever known. But where the hell am I now?

I place my feet on the hardwood floor and pad to the balcony doors when I see my own reflection in a floor-to-ceiling mirror. I look... different.

My hair used to reach below my butt, except someone's chopped it off, leaving it halfway down my back. At least they didn't fuck with the color – it's still a golden blonde like always. Looking down, I realize my nails are done, too. They're longer, almond-shaped and painted pink. I stare at them in wonder, and realize my toes are done in the same manner.

Bile rises in my throat. Someone changed my appearance without my consent. Someone fucked with me while I was out, drugged and abused. My blood chills at the thought. Is this the extent of what they've done, or are they capable of worse?

I hammer my fists against the glass doors of the balcony. The guard gives me a lazy look over his shoulder before returning to his patrol. He doesn't give a damn. He's not going to help me.

I test the door next, but predictably, it's locked. I'm a prisoner. A prisoner Xavier has already started to groom into something different. I feel sick to my stomach.

The door behind me suddenly opens and I spin round, eyes wild as a girl my age or maybe even younger enters the room. She speaks quickly and in a foreign language I don't understand.

"Help me." I rush to her, grabbing her by her arms and begging to be released. "I'm being kept here against my will. They've kidnapped me. You have to help me. I have to get out of here!"

She replies in a quick, melodic voice but I don't understand a word. I groan in frustration, pushing away from her and heading for the door. But before I can step outside, a looming, tall figure appears before me – Xavier. His big hand shoots out and grabs me by the throat.

"Let go of me, you bastard," I hiss at him. "Let me go right now!"

"Or else what?" He smirks, pushing me back inside the room and locking the door from the inside. "You don't have anyone left to save you, little girl. You're at my mercy now."

"Help!" I scream at the top of my voice, but he merely laughs at the sound of my cries.

"You can scream all you want. All these people work for me, nobody's going to help you. And being a dramatic bitch about this will only make life worse for you. I have ways of punishing you."

"Where the hell am I?" I demand.

"Does it matter?" He laughs, nodding to the maid. "I see you've met Adelina. She's been assigned as your maid. Of course, she doesn't speak English. But she'll take care of your looks."

"My looks?" I narrow my eyes at him, burning with hatred. "I don't care about that. I want out of here. I want you brought to justice for what you did to Nana."

"By who, little girl?" His smug smile is unbearable, and I run my hands through my hair in frustration. "You don't have any authority here. And you should do as I say, or I'll make you regret it."

"What did you do to Heath?"

"Again with this bullshit?" He rolls his eyes. "You're really obsessed with the boy, Rain. He's not coming back. He's gone, for fucking good. I own you now."

"But our union," I manage. "We have to be married now that I'm eighteen."

"No," he grins at me. "Change of plans. You'll be marrying me instead."

"You?" I look at him with pure repulsion. "There's no way you can force me to do that."

"I look forward to proving you wrong, little girl." He reaches forward to touch me, but I slap his hand away. His expression hardens and I can tell I've pissed him off, but I don't give a damn. The only way he'll be putting his ring on my finger is if he forces it on my dead fucking body.

"That wasn't very wise," he hisses next. "Remember, you'll be punished for all your transgressions. Remember those nice drugs we pumped inside you to make you all weak?"

I pale, refusing to acknowledge his question. But Xavier already knows he's won.

"Of course you do. We have others, too. Ones that make you obedient. Horny as fuck. Dripping wet. Aggressive. All kinds of shit I can pump into you, all kinds of things I can make you do."

"Don't you dare," I hiss.

He laughs, throwing his head back. "I'd sleep with one eye open if I were you, little girl. Never know when that jab is going to come. Now, are you ready to listen, or do I have to leave you here drugged up for another week?"

"A week?" I ask, horrified by the thought. "I was out for a whole week?"

"Maybe we'll go longer next time." He taps his chin with his forefinger thoughtfully. "Ten days? Two weeks, maybe?"

I fight the urge to spit at him again while fire rages inside me. "You'll pay for what you've done, Xavier."

"Sure." He smiles patronizingly. "You have nobody left to fight your battles, little girl. You're on your fucking own. But not for long, because in just a few short weeks, you're going to become my wife."

"You think it will come true if you say it enough? You can't force me to marry you."

"Of course I can." His attitude is so easygoing it makes me hate him more. As if he doesn't believe for a single second I can fight him on this. "Just fucking watch me, little girl."

We stare at one another while Adelina comes to stand next to us. Sheepishly, she addresses Xavier and he replies in her language, sending her on her way. I can see the guard staring from the balcony, eyes following

Adelina as she leaves the room after tidying up after me.

"As a kindness to you," Xavier goes on. "I'll let you use the library, but that's it, until you learn to behave. And I have a little gift for you, too."

He pulls out two bracelets made of gold. They look more like handcuffs than the jewelry I've seen before.

"I don't want it," I hiss as he reaches for my hand.

"Not your choice." He grabs me by force and attaches the cuffs on both wrists. I pull my arms back and glare at him as he watches me with a look I don't recognize, something amid anger and... affection? "Here's your first test, little girl. I'll leave the door unlocked. You don't leave your room, you get a reward. You do, and it'll be your first taste of what I'm capable of when you piss me off"

I don't answer, just rub the skin where he touched me, trying to get the feeling of his fingers off my skin.

"I'll leave you to it," he says and turns for the door.

"Wait." I hate myself for calling out after him, but I can't help it. I need to know. "You drugged me. You cut my hair. You changed my nails, and my clothes."

"And?" He raises his brows, looking amused, which only makes my stomach turn more.

"Did you... did you..." I swallow. "Did you touch me?"

He doesn't answer, just laughs. "You really don't know anything, do you, little girl?"

With those words, he leaves the room and as promised, doesn't lock the door.

Even though my instincts are telling me to run right away, I need to wait until the guard disappears. He's watching me now, eyes trailing me as I move through the room. Fucking prick.

I feel sick deep down. Xavier's ominous words are making me feel even worse than before. The thought of him taking my clothes off, touching me... it's disgusting, vile. But I have no way of knowing what happened.

In an effort to make myself feel better, I convince myself I would have known if he'd done something to me. And surely, not even Xavier is monstrous enough to rape a girl who's been drugged out of her mind.

I pace the room listlessly. Finally, the guard walks away and nobody replaces him.

Xavier warned me about leaving but I don't have a choice. I have to get out of here, away from this man who took everything from me. Even though I have nowhere to go, even though I have no idea where I am, I have to at least try to get away.

I open the door and stare into the empty hallway. I'm in a large house, with a long gallery hallway that leads to a marble staircase. I must be on the ground floor, though I haven't taken the time to examine the outside world just yet.

"Psst."

I turn around in the direction of the voice. The maid from before, Adelina, stands before me, partially hidden in the shadows and tightly holding on to a duster.

"Don't leave. They'll punish you," she whispers. "It's a test."

"You speak English?" My eyes widen. "Please, you have to help me. Help me get the hell out of here."

"I can't." Her lips form a thin line. "If they knew I spoke English they'd never let me near you. You have to keep it a secret."

I nod eagerly, quickly realizing she might be my only ally in this house. "What happened to Heath?"

"Xavier's ward?" I nod again, but the girl avoids my gaze, shaking her head. "Get back inside, miss. Before they see you."

"Please." I try to grab her but she steps aside, shaking her head.

"Go, before they see you. If you get caught, it will be truly terrible for you."

I'm torn between following her advice and making a run for it. I know her idea makes more sense but the urge to get the hell away is almost too strong to fight. Still, I force myself to walk back into my prison. I close the door and pace the room, wondering whether or not I'm making a mistake.

Adelina brings me food hours later, and only addresses me in the foreign language. I try to beg her for help but she just shakes her head and walks away, her expression nervous.

I pick at the food, worried it might be spiked with drugs. Once I get a few bites down, I blanche as I look up and find Xavier lazily leaning against the door frame.

"You've lasted a few hours," he says. "Congratulations. I shouldn't really give you your reward just yet, but I'm proud of you, little girl."

His nickname for me gives me the creeps but I try not to show it. "What's the reward?"

"Here." He reaches behind his back and hands me a stack of worn paper I know all too well. My eyes widen.

"Heath's letters?"

"Indeed." He watches impassively as I tear into the envelopes. I've read them a thousand times, but right now, they're the only connection I have left to the world Xavier ripped me out of. "I want you to read one to me. Pick your favorite."

I flush. "These are private."

"I read them," he shrugs, making me even angrier. How dare he intrude on my privacy. "They're the ramblings of a love-struck teenager. Nothing new. But I'd like to hear the words from your lips."

"Why?" I demand. "You're just doing this to torture me."

"You catch on quick." He sits down on the loveseat in the room, leaving the door open and taunting me. A way out is so fucking close, and yet we both know the second I make a run for it, Xavier will make me pay for it. "Do go on, little girl. I don't have all day to torture you."

"And if I refuse?"

"I was hoping you'd ask." He runs a hand through his dark, slicked back hair before lazily reaching into his pocket and pulling out a phone. I swallow. He could call for help now, but of course he won't. Instead, he presses a button, powering an electric current to shock my body.

I scream in frustration, trying to get away when he shocks me again. I quickly realize the cuffs are doing this, but as I struggle to take them off, Xavier merely laughs at my misfortune.

"The only way they come off is if you saw them off your wrists," he tells me. "Now fucking read the letter, I'm losing my patience."

I force myself to pick a letter from the stack, still recovering from the cruel torture he just put me through. My voice shakes as I begin to read, redness creeping into my cheeks. This is next level embarrassing.

"Goldilocks," I begin. "Today must be your seventeenth birthday. I hope you get the letter in time so you can read it on your special day. Only one year separates us from our marriage. I often wonder if you remember me, if you think about me, if you replay our kiss in your mind..."

"Keep going," Xavier barks. "It sounds so much better coming from you."

I swallow, continuing, "And if you wish you could see me again before we say I do. I certainly do. I cannot tell you much of what's going on here, as you know. And I find it difficult to talk about my feelings, especially when it comes to you, Goldilocks."

"I always hated that nickname," Xavier mutters, humiliating me further.

"That's the end of the letter." I put it back on the stack.

"Is it?" He smirks, reaching into his pocket and bringing out another page scribbled with Heath's handwriting.

"Where did you get that?"

"He wrote so much, we couldn't send it all," Xavier mutters. "Too much sensitive information, you see."

I grab the page from his hand and he doesn't argue. My eyes scan Heath's scribbled handwriting and words jump out at me.

Guardian. Secrets. Liar. Afraid. Plans. Sinister. Tell your nana to be careful.

Before I can make sense of it all, Xavier takes the page and the rest of the letters and walks over to the fireplace in my bedroom. He carefully stacks them inside and lights a match.

"Don't," I hiss. "Don't you fucking dare."

"You need to accept it's over," he says, tossing the match into the hearth. "This was the only way to teach you."

"No!" I throw myself at the fireplace and snatch a letter from the flames. Xavier curses and pulls me back. Sobs wrack my body as the letter turns to blackened ash in my hand. I drop it on the floor, watching my past crumble.

"Stupid little girl," Xavier says with a smirk on his face. "So fucking breakable you are, Rain... I'm going to have my fun with you."

Chapter Three

RAIN

1 WEEK LATER

I've been Xavier Gunn's captive for two weeks now, one of which I spent unconscious.

Every day, I see Adelina who still refuses to speak English to me. I see Xavier too – I'm forced to have dinner with him daily, but he barely addresses me while we eat. We're joined by guards most of the time, and I never get the chance to plan my escape. The cuffs prevent me from running, and I soon realize the house is a beachfront property atop a cliff, with only a long, winding road as a way of escape. A road I couldn't bear to walk on in this heat – if I even got far with the fucking cuffs.

Yesterday at dinner, Xavier told me I would attend an event in the house today. One with guests. This fills me with hope – perhaps I can finally find someone who speaks my language and can help me get away from this hell.

I spend the day with Adelina, getting ready for dinner, with a guard watching us closely. Adelina washes, blow-dries and styles my hair, and for the first time, I have my makeup done by her careful hand. I'm amazed by the pots and pans that hold color and beauty, but I have no time to dwell on the miracle of makeup. I'm determined to walk away from here tonight.

Adelina presents me with a dress. It's blood red, structured, with one sleeve and a deeply cut neckline that frames my chest. The dress leaves nothing to the imagination, clinging to my body tightly. I fucking hate Xavier for making me wear this humiliating outfit in front of his guests.

A pair of black leather stilettos completes the look. I don't even recognize myself. I'm someone else now. The girl with golden hair died along with Nana.

I can hear the guests arriving outside, but I haven't been allowed to leave my room yet.

I'm anxious, nervously pacing as I wait for the door to open. I'm locked in again, my test apparently over for now, and as much as I hate myself for it, I seem to have passed it with flying colors.

Finally, the door opens and Adelina appears, nervously motioning for me to come forward. I rush to her side and she escorts me away from my hallway for the first time.

The house we're in is enormous, modern and visibly expensive. Everything I touch is marble, expensive wood or crystal. Beautiful artwork decorates the walls and modern sculptures are artfully placed in the interior of the house.

Adelina leads me into a grand hall where the view of the beach below is beautiful. I can hear voices now, and more and more guards appear as Adelina escorts me into a grand dining hall.

There are at least a hundred people seated at a long table. At the head, there is Xavier, wearing a crisp, expensively cut tux and a smug expression. His eyes meet mine and he motions me forward. Nobody looks up from their meal as I take a seat to the left of Xavier.

My heart hammers in my chest painfully. I want to scream for help. I want to get the hell out of here. But the longer I look at Xavier's guests, the closer I am to a horrible realization.

There are mostly men at the table, but those who are accompanied by women stand out. I look at the rare few women at the table. They're all wearing the same cuffs I am.

My blood runs cold.

I stare at my plate without an appetite. Course after course is placed in front of me and I don't touch any of them. While the rest of the guests chatter among themselves in a mix of English and the foreign language I still don't recognize, Xavier seems focused on one thing only – me.

I can feel his burning gaze but I don't acknowledge it. I don't even look at him. He doesn't deserve my attention.

There's a small commotion a couple of seats down, and I blanche as one of the suit-clad men slaps his companion across the face, fucking hard.

I hurriedly glance at Xavier, muttering, "Aren't you going to do something? He just hit her!"

He grins in response, not saying a word. I fucking hate him.

More courses are brought out, until finally dessert is served and the meal is over. As the waiting staff clears the table, Xavier addresses me again.

"I'm glad you're here for the big event," he says. "We can begin now."

The table quietens down as a screen unfolds on an empty wall before us. I glance between Xavier and the guests, not understanding what's happening. But then a projector clicks on, and Xavier gets up, addressing everyone.

"Thank you for coming. I hope you're as excited as I am to welcome my fiancée Rain Ferrell into our world. Let's watch a little introductory film about Rain, shall we?"

My eyes scan his face for an explanation, but the smug smirk is firmly back in place as he sits back down, nodding in the direction of the screen.

"You won't want to miss this, Rain."

I turn my attention to the screen, not knowing what to expect. An image starts up, the video playing out in slow motion. It's me, but I don't remember this, don't remember any of it. And that makes my blood run cold.

I watch my body being stashed into the shiny black car. I watch as they load me onto an airplane. I watch as guards and Xavier make fun of me while I'm passed out, and my eyes burn with unshed tears.

I'm splayed out on an airplane seat, my dress riding up obscenely. My eyes are half-open, heavy-lidded and spinning every once in a while. I glance around me nervously, not knowing what to think of this embarrassing display, but everyone's eyes are glued to the screen. Everyone's, except Xavier's – because he's staring right at me, smirking and motioning for me to continue watching.

I return my attention to the video. Xavier walks into the frame and grins at the camera before pulling out a pair of scissors. I watch, horrified, as he cuts into my dress, tearing it down the middle. Nana's dress, one she sewed painstakingly slowly while I slept in my cot. All her effort is gone, wasted, turned to a mockery as Xavier discards the torn fabric and exposes my bare body.

I close my eyes firmly, willing the image to go away. But no matter what I do, the proof is right in front of me. This really happened. They really did this to me. And there's nothing I can do now to change it.

I watch, flushing deeply as he exposes my body to the camera. The person filming comes in close, getting a good shot of my drugged face, my body lolling to the side as he films me in high definition, from my hardened nipples to the wet thatch of blonde hair between my legs.

The need to hurt Xavier is strong, but I know I'll be stopped the moment I try to attack him. Instead, my nails dig painfully into my palms as I continue to watch his assault. He touches me, obscenely running his hands over my naked body, twisting, pinching my nipples. He laughs at the camera and invites it closer, showing me off like I'm a fucking trophy. He parts my pussy lips, showing my wetness for the camera, swiping a finger up my center and sucking it into his mouth while he laughs and laughs and laughs.

I shoot up in my seat, glaring at the guests.

"Is no one going to say something?" I demand. "Nobody wants to help me? He's abusing me and you're all part of it!"

"Dearest Rain, do sit down," Xavier tells me calmly. "You haven't even seen the best part yet."

I refuse to sit down, but one of the guards shoves me hard, and I stumble before doing as I'm told. Tears of frustration and shame burn my eyes, demanding retribution for what Xavier did to me.

Shifting my attention back to the video, I watch as not only Xavier, but several of his guards touch me, humiliate me and do things to my unconscious body that make me want to weep. But I hold back the tears. I have to. The moment the first drop falls, I'll break down completely.

The sight of it is sickening. Bile lurches in the pit of my stomach, threatening to make me sick, but I force it down. I will not give this fucked up man the satisfaction of knowing what he's done to my mind. He may have taken advantage of my body, but I'll never let him break me into submission. Not under any circumstance.

The image on the screen changes. Now I'm in the bedroom I woke up in, my body still lifeless and limp. Xavier appears on the frame, fixing the camera that must be in the room, one I haven't noticed. I fucking hate the bastard for putting me under constant surveillance. He's going to pay for this.

I watch as my naked body is washed carefully by Xavier. At least he isn't too rough. But what stings more is that all this truly happened even though I don't remember a second of it.

After he's done wiping me down, Xavier injects me with something, grinning to himself. Then, he sits in an armchair and crosses his legs, placing his hands behind his head and waiting.

Confused, I knit my brows together and glance at Xavier sitting at the head of the table. "What did you do to me, you sick fuck?"

"Keep watching, little girl," he mutters.

I want to deny him the pleasure of my shocked expression, so I force myself to remain stoic as I shift my attention back to the camera feed. My eyes fly open and I pick myself up with a low, throaty moan. I can't believe what I'm seeing. I can't believe I don't remember this – any of it. It's utterly shameful.

With horror, I watch myself tearing at my body, my fingers going between my legs, playing with my pussy, twisting my nipples. What the hell is happening?

"What did you inject me with?" I demand from Xavier. "You sick monster. How could you do that to me? Somebody help me!"

But a look at the guests seated around the dining table reveals what I already knew – none of these people fucking care. They love watching me get abused. In fact, some of their companions are now on their knees, massaging, sucking and caressing the men's cocks.

Disgusted, I pick myself up. As much as I want to know what Xavier did to me, I'm not going to keep watching this. "Fuck you, Xavier. Fuck you, fuck you, fuck you."

With a click of his fingers, Xavier brings forward a guard who shoves me back down on the chair. Two others make quick work of tying my hands and feet to the chair's legs. I struggle against them with no use. They easily overpower me.

"You can't fucking force me to watch this," I hiss at Xavier. "You can't make me!"

I shut my eyes tightly, trying to block out the sound of my own moans on the video.

But a slap to my right cheek slams me back to reality, and I'm forced to stare at Xavier as he hisses, "You will not disobey. You will watch, and you will fucking take what I give you. If not, I'll fucking hook your eyes back and make you."

I want to spit in his face, but fear holds me frozen like a statue. Unmoving, I shift my attention back to the screen. I don't recognize myself. I don't want to recognize myself.

The girl on the screen drops to her knees and crawls to Xavier. She buries her face in his crotch and he laughs at her helplessness.

What the fuck did he inject into me? These drugs are poison. Horrifying, terrifying poison running through my veins and making me into this savage animal I don't recognize.

I close my eyes again, but the next moment Xavier is behind me, forcing me to look at the screen and holding my head in place.

"Look," he hisses against my ear, sending goosebumps all over my skin. "Watch as you debase yourself, little girl."

With horror, I watch myself getting on top of his cock and sliding it inside me with an animalistic moan.

My virginity... Did I really do this? Did they drug me up and force my body into this? Did they make me lose my last shred of innocence to this vile man?

Something breaks inside me, irreparable harm being done to my mind and soul. I don't know how to escape, and up until now, I was determined to run. But now, everything changes. And as Xavier holds on to me, forcing me to watch the horror show before me, I know I've lost the war.

"Look," he smirks against my shoulder, licking my skin and making me shudder. "Look at your virginity all over my dick, little girl. I didn't even have to force you..."

I start to sob then, unable to resist the tears anymore.

"Keep watching," Xavier whispers, taking a step back. But his prying hands are quickly replaced by other men. Guards and guests alike touch me, grope me, pinch me, bruise me. I let myself get lost in the sobs, pretending I don't see what's on the screen, pretending this is happening to anybody but me. It can't be real. If I wish hard enough, I can will it to not be real.

But I can't take my eyes off the screen. I have to watch this, to know what he did to me, to know why I hate him. And I watch his fingers disappearing into the hole between my legs just as Xavier pushes a guard aside and does the same thing with me in the present.

"I know everything about you," he tells me. "I know how sensitive your nipples are. I know what makes you come."

A ragged breath escapes my lips. He's trying to do it, trying to give me an orgasm I don't want. My body ignites with hatred for this monster.

I struggle, but he orders two guards to hold me down. I'm forced to take his fingers inside me, fucking me in perfect rhythm to the image on the screen. Hot tears of humiliation burn my cheeks as something breaks inside me. I'm going to have my vendetta over this man. Not now. Not soon. But some day.

He brings me closer and closer to an orgasm and I soon realize I won't be able to fight it.

And when I come, it's in tune with my image on the screen. Both of us explode, both of us soak Xavier's fingers. The only difference is that on the screen, my face is overtaken by pleasure while in reality, I wear a mask of pain and hatred.

The hands traveling over my body disappear into nothingness. The image of my body being ravaged by a man I hate on the screen fades. All I see now is a pair of slanted, charcoal eyes.

I focus on them. Imagine every detail, every light fleck, every shade of his emotion in those eyes. I recall his letters, his neat and precise handwriting, his carefully picked words. I force myself to remember Heath Gunn and cling to his memory, the last thing that tethers me to the world I knew... before this.

Before Xavier.

Before my life ended before my very eyes.

As I force myself to detach my mind from my body, I feel something else being forced on me. I open my eyes and see it – a gaudy, huge diamond on a thin platinum band encircling my ring finger.

I look up into Xavier's eyes, feeling my blood run cold.

"For better or for worse, little girl," he tells me darkly. "I own you now."

Chapter Four

HEATH

I DON'T REMEMBER A life before this one.

I know there must've been one, because my memories don't extend that far back. Once upon a time, I was something other than a fucked up, twisted monster serving the dark side. Perhaps I was a boy, a boy who had parents, a loving family, and friends.

There is one thing I remember. Every night as I lie in my prison cell, I force myself to remember the only thing that's left of my life before the cartel. The only thing that ties me to something other than this dark dungeon, the smell of blood, sweat, and fucking.

I remember the girl with the golden hair the color of shining wheat caught in the sunset.

Her bright blue eyes. Her sweet face, a light complexion peppered with freckles. Her slightly crooked front teeth that only made her more beautiful. And her hair, her glorious hair. I can never forget that, not even when they pump me full of the drugs that destroy my mind.

I lie on my back in the cell that has been my home for as long as I can remember. My fingertips travel over the rough expanse of the wall, scratching lines into it with my nails.

Surely life wasn't always like this. Surely, I have something left to fight for. Surely there's something, someone, worth saving at the end of this journey.

The cell door opens and I'm on my feet in a second, mouth open in a snarl, ready to snap at the guards as they throw a figure at me. But before I can smash my fist in the broken figure's jaw, I realize who it is.

"L," I grunt. "What the fuck have they done to you?"

All I get in return is a painful groan. I glare at the guards who are already retreating from the cage, careless about the pain they've caused.

"Fucking bastards," I roar. "Give us medicine! Give us our fucking freedom!"

Only the sound of their laughter waits for me in their wake. They lock the cage and take their spots guarding the space, chatting among themselves and not giving a shit about us.

I grunt as I drag L's unmoving body to the bunk bed in the corner of the room. It takes some effort to lift him onto the lower bed. We always fight about who gets to sleep on this one, but today, there's no doubt he needs this more than I do.

My hands shake as they hover over the man who's the closest thing I have to family in here. He's like my brother, with me through all the shit the cartel has put me through. We've been there for each other, patching up the wounds, watching them scar and pucker while months went by. It could've been years for all I know. My head is so fucked from the poison they pump into me, I have no fucking idea.

"Man, don't leave me hanging," I mutter as I check the extent of L's wounds. He's bleeding profusely from an ugly cut on his side. His forehead's bleeding too, and the bruising on his torso is so bad I already know he's broken at least two ribs. "I can't stay here without you. I can't fight this battle on my own."

Finally, a voice cuts through the silence and I grin as L mutters, "You fucking wish you could get rid of me, prick."

"Do you need water?" I ask, and he nods, wincing as he tries to move on the bed.

I rush to the cage doors, banging on them. "Water! Medicine!"

The guards ignore me. I'm used to it, and I'd probably give up if it weren't for my brother in this hole. But this time, I'm propelled by the need to help L, and I rattle the bars, fucking roaring for attention.

"Would you fucking shut up?" one of the guards snarls. He's real fucking brave when he's on the other side of this cage. I still remember biting him badly enough he needed stitches only days ago when he got too close. "Shut the fuck up!"

"Water! Medicine," I demand. "Fucking *now*."

With a groan, he picks himself up from his station, coming closer with a plastic bottle of water. He's fucking loving this, I can tell from his twisted grin. He empties the water bottle into his mouth, letting precious liquid drip to the floor before tossing it at me. I make a desperate grab for the plastic and both guards laugh at my effort.

"Medicine," I hiss next. "He's bleeding, his ribs are broken, he needs painkillers."

"He can take it," the other guard smirks before walking closer. "Take this."

He tosses a tiny packet on the floor of the cell and I scramble to grab it, hoping for pills, even an injection of their fucked up poison – anything to dull my brother's pain. But as I open the packet to the sound of the guards cackling, I realize it's a shitty sewing kit.

I spit on the floor, swearing to myself I'll rip their throats out when I get the chance. But I'll be stronger with L by my side, so I have to help him first.

There's only one way for me to get water into the empty plastic bottle, and I'm already fucking dreading it. As I fill the bottle from the toilet bowl in the corner in the room, knowing they won't give us anything else for days, I curse inwardly. I'm having a rare moment of lucidity, one where I can remember more than I usually do.

Golden hair.

Blue eyes.

I shake my head to get the thought out. Not telling L where I got the water, I pour some into his shaking mouth. He's losing consciousness, dropping in and out as I get to work on the nasty cut decorating his side.

My hands shake. I've never been good at this shit. The needle pricks L's skin but he doesn't even flinch – a clear sign he's more fucked up than I thought. I'm working with a shitty needle and the thread barely holds it all together. I know it must hurt like hell, but luckily, L's passed the fuck out from the pain.

The guards watch me with impassive faces, not offering help or saying a word about what they're making me do. At least they ain't fucking laughing – it's a welcome change to the endless sound of their snickering at our misfortune.

I don't stop until I've stitched L up. His groans and grunts are making me feel even angrier at the world.

I crawl on the upper bunk bed later on, knowing I have to catch at least a wink of sleep before they come for us again. Given L's condition, I'm guessing I'll be the next one dragged into the cage.

That's what they do to us here. Inject us with adrenaline and their messed up drugs, and force us to fight. Sometimes each other, if we aren't lucky, sometimes other men we know nothing about. They place bets on us and discard our bodies when we inevitably bite the dust. There used to be five men in this cage, but now it's only me and L.

L doesn't remember his name, except the first letter. He clings to that now, just like I cling to the memory of the golden-haired girl.

I lie on my back on the upper bunk, trying to catch a wink of sleep but the blaring sounds of the guards' TV doesn't let me. By the time they appear in front of the cage again, I'm already up and ready to pounce.

They have someone with them. A frail looking girl with black hair and an olive complexion. She's pretty but too innocent looking. I catch her when one of the pricks pushes her against me.

"Fuck her," he orders.

I look at the terrified girl in my arms, then back at the guard, shaking my head. "No."

"No?" He laughs, calling his bald friend over. "You hear this guy? Says he won't do it."

"Oh yeah?" The bald man smirks. "Luckily, we have ways of making you obey."

I glare at them, pushing the girl aside. She stumbles as I approach the bars, but before I can make a move to grab one of them, an electric current flows through my body, shocking me. One of the bastards fucking tased me like I'm a goddamn animal.

I stumble back as the cage opens and one of them walks inside. I'm too stunned to fight as he plunges a thick, painful syringe into my neck, releasing another vial of poison. I've been through this enough times to know what's going to happen, but it still doesn't make it easier.

These pricks have developed drugs that make them able to control me. Because as soon as their poison gets into my veins, there's no fighting it. It turns me into a ravenous, bloodthirsty fucking monster and there's no way in hell I can fight it.

I slump back against the bars as I feel the drug taking effect, roaring at the burn in my veins. The raven-haired girl's eyes widen as she realizes what's about to happen, and she throws herself at the locked door, banging her fists against the bars and begging the guards to let her out. But no such luck. The pricks have already pulled up chairs and are watching us with darkened, lustful expressions. And I can't hold myself back for much longer.

With a growl, I pick myself up from the floor. My predatory eyes find the girl who looks fucking terrified, but I'm past the point of acknowledging her fear. I smell the air. I can smell her. I can fucking smell her pussy, her trepidation working like an aphrodisiac as every nerve ending in my body demands to be satisfied.

The poison is flowing freely, pumping my muscles, engorging my cock into a painful rod between my legs. Primal instincts kick in. A part of me is still there, present in my mind but having no fucking control of my body. Pushed into the darkest corner of my thoughts, I watch myself grab for the girl.

I make a game of grabbing, letting go, grabbing again. It's like a cat playing with a mouse for its own amusement, always knowing it can overpower its prey. And when it looks like she'll slip away again, my hand wraps firmly around her forearm, making her scream bloody fucking murder.

Everything fades into a red mist that covers my eyes, making me see her as nothing but a set of three holes for me to fuck, abuse and fill. There's nothing that can be done for the poor girl now.

I rip off her clothes, throwing the tattered remains on the ground. Her skin isn't the way I remember. Her hair isn't the way I remember. But my body thinks it's *her*, attacking the girl savagely. I nip and bite at her skin, bruising her and drawing blood, unable to stop myself. She starts to sob as I pin her against the bars, forgetting about the guards, seeing only the piece of flesh in my arms. The need to tear her apart fucking hurts, and yet I can't resist it.

My cock forces itself inside her. She's a virgin – if it weren't obvious by her tight little cunt, it's proven by the trace of blood on my cock. Probably another one they stole to train for the cartel. In the coming months, her pussy will be used, abused, filled and beaten until she finally succumbs to the life these men want for her. She'll be a toy, nothing more. And her lesson begins right here, with me.

I tear through her, claiming untouched territory, ripping through her as the drug courses through my veins, rendering me almost mindless. This is all I am now, a man who wants pleasure, a man who wants to empty his dick into the first unfortunate set of holes to cross his path.

In the back of my mind, the boy I locked away breaks again.

In the cage, though, my body grows stronger, more violent with every thrust of my powerful hips into the girl's pussy. I fuck her like the monster I am, without mercy, without taking a second to breathe.

My fist grips her hair, the strands falling between my fingers as I furrow my brows at them. Not the color I remember, too dark. I grab her by the neck and she shrieks as I force her to look at me. Gray eyes, not the cornflower blue I remember so well. It's wrong, all so fucking wrong, yet I can't stop it. I need to fill her, come in her. The drug in my blood is making me lose my mind, pumping, fucking, groaning, turning into a monster as I bury my cock deeper and deeper inside her, taking, stealing, taking advantage.

The guards in front of us have been forgotten. I'm too preoccupied by the girl's tightness to care about her screams of pain. All I care about is my dick, growing thicker, angrier, harder and harder between my legs with every thrust of my hips.

"Stop!" the girl screams. "Please, stop, you're hurting me, please don't do this..."

But even she must realize it's all in vain – she's not addressing me, but instead the guards in front of the cage who smirk, beating their own cocks watching us. They'll probably take turns on her after, not stopping until they've both filled her with their filthy loads.

She doesn't even know what she's in for. Her world's about to get even more fucked up once I finish.

I can feel the fight leaving her body as I break her more and more. She's a helpless puppet, no longer able to stand on her own. But I'm not done yet, fuck no. Not until she passes out. They usually have to drag me off the girls...

I lower her body to the ground and keep pumping inside her. I still can't see through the red mist, but I can clearly see she's not the right girl. Not the one with golden hair and blue eyes. Someone else – someone I don't know, someone I don't want. Except my body is unstoppable.

As my friend lies unconscious on the bed behind me, I fill the girl with my seed, watching it drip out of her pussy as I take a step back to admire my work. A bloodthirsty smile lights up my darkened features. I watch her with a sick, brutal satisfaction and lick my lips at the sight.

There's a memory of golden hair, like strands of tinsel and wheat, against my fingers.

There's a glimpse of blue eyes, bright blue, painfully blue.

There's her face. Her beautiful, young, innocent face.

And then there's a flash of a name.

Rain.

Rain.

Rain.

I stumble back, running my hands through my hair in a desperate attempt to get the thought to stay. But the guards must see what's happening, because one of them plunges another injection into me, this time in my thigh, making me tumble backward as another burn sweeps through my body.

Rain.

Rain.

Rain.

No, no, *no*. I'm forgetting. I'm slipping away. All I can feel is the painful burn, the hardness that makes me roar again. The girl on the floor scrambles away, but she's too slow again, and my possessive arms grab her, flip her over and pin her the fuck down.

"Please!" she screams. "Don't hurt me!"

I don't listen to her. I do exactly what she's most afraid of. I become her living nightmare, the man that will haunt her dreams until she dies at the hands of these monsters.

And all the while, I force myself to remember the name, through the haze, through the poison, through the pain. That's all that matters, clinging on to that one memory, that one thing that will keep me human, not turn me into a monster.

Rain.

Rain.

Rain.

I'm coming for you, Rain.

<hr>

TO BE CONTINUED

Heath and Rain's story continues in The Wife Breaker. Preorder now!

Coming Soon

Thank you for reading The Bride Thief! If you enjoyed it, I'd love to read your review. It means so much to me.

Next up, continue Rain and Heath's story in the first book of this dark, enemies-to-lovers arranged marriage duet with book one, The Wife Breaker.

Also By Kendall Hawkins

DARK VOWS DUET

#0.5 The Bride Thief

#1 The Wife Breaker

#2 The Widow Maker

About Kendall Hawkins

Kendall Hawkins is an emerging author of heart-twisting romance.

Embracing her dark side brought Kendall to write dark romance that leaves you breathless. Since she was a little girl, Kendall has cheered for the villain to get the girl, loved the dark side and adored shocking plot twists. Now, her love of enticing stories fills her days with villainous heroes and the passionate women they love.

Kendall spends her time writing, sculpting and creating in any way she can. Addicted to art, Kendall continues to pour her talents out on any medium available – be it a blank page, a canvas or modelling clay.

Learn more about Kendall:
Newsletter
Instagram

Facebook group

www.ingramcontent.com/pod-product-compliance
Lightning Source LLC
Chambersburg PA
CBHW031756150726

47989CB00006B/2749